ARCTIC OCEAN

N

NORTH
AMERICA

NORTH
ATLANTIC
OCEAN

EUROPE

Baltic
Sea

Volga

Danube

ASIA

Black
Sea

Caspian
Sea

Mississippi

Mediterranean Sea

Yangtze

PACIFIC
OCEAN

Caribbean
Sea

AFRICA

Nile

Red Sea

Ganges

Amazon

PACIFIC
OCEAN

SOUTH
AMERICA

INDIAN
OCEAN

AUSTRALIA

Murray-Darling

SOUTH
ATLANTIC
OCEAN

0   1000 2000 Km

0   500 1000 Miles

SOUTHERN OCEAN

Shiny the Sea Star

Surfs the Seas and Finds

a Mississippi River Paddlewheel Boat

Written and illustrated by
Cleopatra B. Alexander

Also by Cleopatra B. Alexander

Shiny the Sea Star Surfs the Seas and Finds
a Yangtze River Dragon

Shiny la Estrella de Mar, Surfea los Mares y Encuentra
un Dragón en el Río Yangtze

Shiny la Estrella de Mar, Surfea los Mares y Encuentra
un Barco a Vapor de Ruedas del Río Mississippi

Shiny the Sea Star
Surfs the Seas and Finds
a Mississippi River Paddlewheel Boat

Written and illustrated by
Cleopatra B. Alexander

WaveRider Press
Evanston, IL

Cleopatra Bugelas Alexander

www.shinyseastar.com

First Edition
Designed by María Vélez

Library of Congress Control Number: 2017902937
ISBN: 978-0-9968666-1-3
eBook ISBN: 978-0-9968666-5-1
Printed in the United States of America
WaveRider Press
www.waveriderpress.com

For Elizabeth and
Christopher
Love Ya, Mom

"Just as the waters of the Mississippi
merge with the Gulf of Mexico
and eventually with each ocean,
the wish for peace and happiness
extends from the banks of
the Mississippi across the globe."

— *Hannibal Courier-Post*, May 21, 2016

Shiny the Sea Star loves playing with boats under the Santa Monica Pier, where he lives.

He has a Sail Boat that zips across the water when he WHOOSHES on the sail.

He has a Motor Boat that, with a big push, can pass the Sail Boat as Shiny shouts, VROOM! VROOM!

He even has a Dragon Boat that he got on his visit to the Yangtze River in China.

10

One day, Shiny visits the Library and sees a poster that has a picture of a boat he had never seen before.

Ms. Muriel, Ms. Muriel, what kind boat is that? he asks his favorite Dolphin Librarian.

Why, Shiny, that's a Paddlewheel Boat. Paddlewheel Boats go up and down the Mississippi River, she answered.

M-I-S-S-I-S-S-I-P-P-I! M-I-S-S-I-S-S-I-P-P-I! M-I-S-S-I-S-S-I-P-P-I!

Shiny shouts, running home to his Mom.

Please, please, please, Mom, may I go to the M-I-S-S-I-S-S-I-P-P-I River to find a Paddlewheel Boat for my collection?

Well, Shiny, you were careful on your adventure to the Yangtze River, so yes, you may go to the Mississippi River.

Go see Handy the Octopus at his Adventure Store, and ask for directions and supplies.

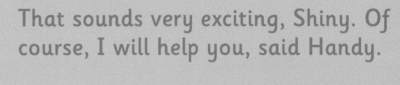

Hello, Handy, Mom said I could go to the M-I-S-S-I-S-S-I-P-P-I River to find a Paddlewheel Boat for my collection. Please help me get ready for my next adventure.

That sounds very exciting, Shiny. Of course, I will help you, said Handy.

Let's start packing your Starpack.

Here's a map, a box of your favorite Kelp O's cereal, and a picture of your home, under the Santa Monica Pier.

13

Here's the most important thing of all, Shiny, your compass.

LISTEN UP! You have a long way to go and your compass will help show you the way.

It will always point north, and when you know that, you can figure out the other directions: south, east and west.

YOU MUST NEVER LOSE IT!!!

Now, let's talk about your trip.
We live under the Santa Monica Pier,

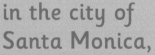 

Mississippi River

in the city of
Santa Monica,

in the state of
California,

in the United States
of America.

The Mississippi River is in the United States of America.

It is very, very long. It is 2,320 miles long!

It starts in the state of Minnesota, passes by 8 states and ends in the state of Louisiana, near the city of New Orleans.

That's where you will find your Paddlewheel Boat, Shiny.

United States of America

If you could drive a car, Shiny, you could take a very famous road called Route 66 to get there.

Route 66 ends right here at the Santa Monica Pier and starts in the city of Chicago, which has one of the tallest buildings in the world.

Chicago

Santa Monica

St. Louis

Route 66 also will take you to the city of St. Louis, which is right on the Mississippi River.

There is a very beautiful and very big Arch right along the river. It is called the Gateway to the West.

Since you are a Sea Star and cannot drive a car, you have to take a water road. That's no problem because the whole world is connected by water.

You can hop on a wave here at the Santa Monica Pier in the Pacific Ocean and surf your way to rivers all over the world, including the Mississippi River.

Remember:
The ocean has motion,
which moves all around,
the continents all seven,
where rivers abound!

Here's the map with your route, said Handy. Don't worry, it looks harder than it is. The MOST IMPORTANT thing you will need is your COMPASS!

Number 1:
Surf south all the way to the end of South America. Boats can use a short-cut through the Panama Canal, but it's not for Sea Stars.

Number 2:
Turn east at the very tip of South America, at Cape Horn.

Number 3:
Turn north and surf all the way to the state of Florida, at the tip of the United States.

Number 4:
Surf west to the Mississippi River.

My friend, Archie the Turtle, will meet you there, in the city of New Orleans.

OK, Shiny, time to start your adventure. All set?

You bet! shouted Shiny.

Remember: DO NOT LOSE YOUR COMPASS!!!

I'll ask my Seagull Travel Team to tell Archie you're coming. Don't worry, I'll tell your Mom you'll be home soon.

Quick! Jump on this wave!

Shiny surfs all the way to the tip of South America and then, TROUBLE! Suddenly, a giant wave splashes over him and he falls through the water!

His Starpack is soaked! His compass flies off! Help me! Help me! Shiny shouts to a huge Whale that is swimming by.

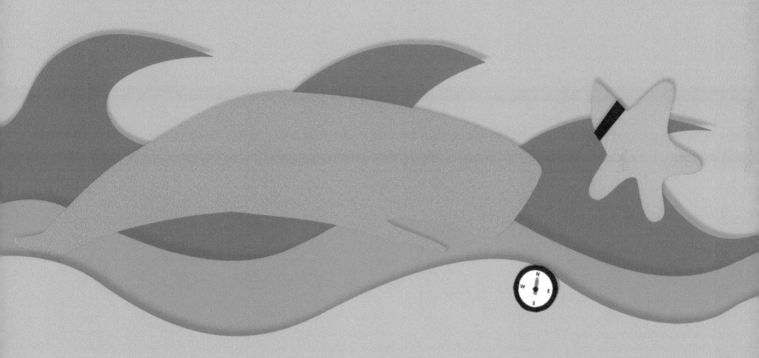

Whoa! growls the Whale. Where do you think you're going?

Oh, Sir, said Shiny.

Call me, Rover, said the Whale, as he scooped Shiny up onto his back. Who are you? What's your problem?

Oh, Rover, I'm Shiny the Sea Star and I'm trying to get to the Mississippi River. I lost my compass and I will be lost FOREVER!

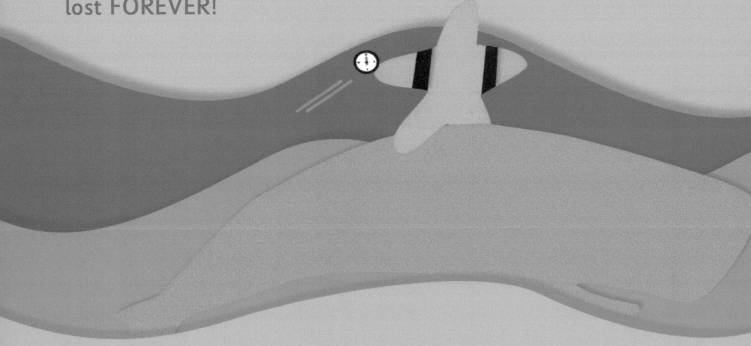

Relax, Shiny, here's your compass. I saw it slip off your arm and saved it. Catch!

Oh, thank you, Rover! Archie the Turtle is waiting for me on the River.

I'm happy you're meeting a friend, Shiny. I'll take you to the Gulf of Mexico where you can jump into the Mississippi.

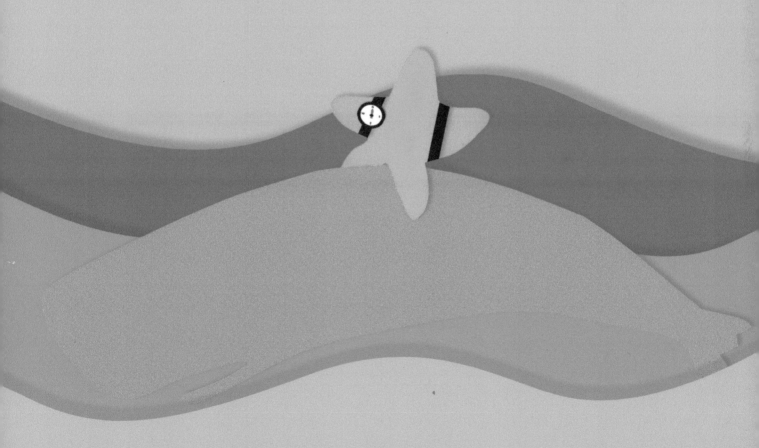

Archie! Archie! Where are you?

Here I am, Shiny, shouted Archie.

Bye, Rover, said Shiny. Thank you for saving me!

Welcome to the Mighty Mississippi River, Shiny, said Archie.

Hi, Archie! Handy sent me to find a toy Paddlewheel Boat. He says hello!

Well, Shiny, you came to just the right place. Paddlewheel Boats have gone up and down the Mississippi River for years. See? There's one over there. It's called the Mark Twain, after the famous book writer.

The Mississippi is a very big river, Shiny. It starts in the state of Minnesota and ends in the state of Louisiana.

Special boats called Barges travel the river carrying all kinds of things people need: wood for building boats, paper to make books, and grain to make cereal and bread.

Tow Boats push these Barges along the river. One Tow Boat can push 15 Barges all hooked together!

You've come to New Orleans, one of the most famous cities on the Mississippi River.

New Orleans is a very old city. It really started growing in 1718.

We have many colorful buildings. Many were built by people whose families crossed the Atlantic Ocean from France and Spain.

A very busy part of the city is called the French Quarter.

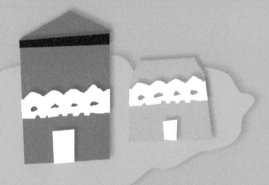

We also have a very famous school, Tulane University.

Archie, listen! I hear music!

Yes, Shiny, you came at the right time. Our Mardi Gras Parade is just beginning. We have one every year. Bands play our famous New Orleans music. It's called Jazz.

People dress in costumes and ride on giant floats.
They throw beads to everyone who comes to watch.

Here comes a float now! Quick, Shiny! Catch some beads!

Yea! I caught some! I caught some! shouted Shiny.

I'm going to give these beads to Ms. Muriel, my favorite Librarian. I still need to find a Mississippi River Paddlewheel Boat for my collection, Archie.

Don't worry, Shiny. We're on our way to my favorite carnival. My friend, Sam, is in charge of the Ring Toss game. You throw a ring over a row of toy boats, and, if the ring lands around one of the boats, you can take it home. I'm sure you will win a Paddlewheel Boat to take home.

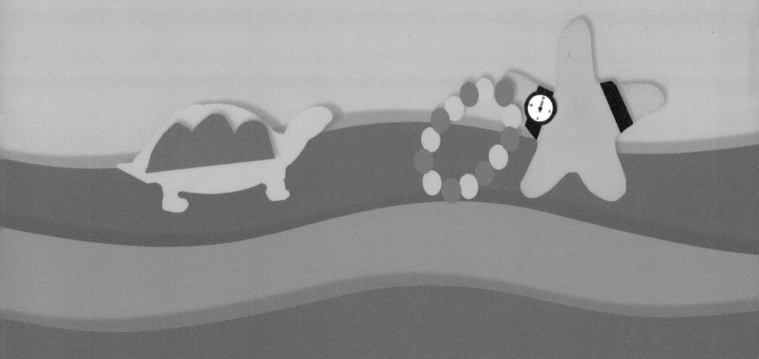

Hi, Sam, calls Archie.

I'm here with my new friend, Shiny the Sea Star.
He wants to try to win one of your Paddlewheel Boats.

Welcome to New Orleans, Shiny, said Sam.

See that row of boats? You can try to win a Dragon Boat, a Sail Boat or a Paddlewheel Boat. All you have to do is throw a ring around one of them and it is yours!

Well, I already have a Dragon Boat and I already have a Sail Boat. I came for a Paddlewheel Boat, Sam.

Then just aim for that one, Shiny.

Shiny throws the ring – not too far, not too close and not too crooked.

Oh My Stars! shouts Shiny. I did it! I won my Paddlewheel Boat! Now, I'm ready to go home.

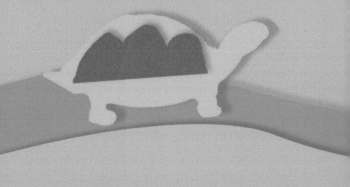

That's great, Shiny, said Sam. Have a good trip home!

Bye, Sam! Thank you!

OK, Shiny, now follow me along the Mississippi. Then, you can jump on a good wave and start surfing home, called Archie.

1! 2! 3! Jump Shiny! Say hi to Handy!

Thank you, Archie!

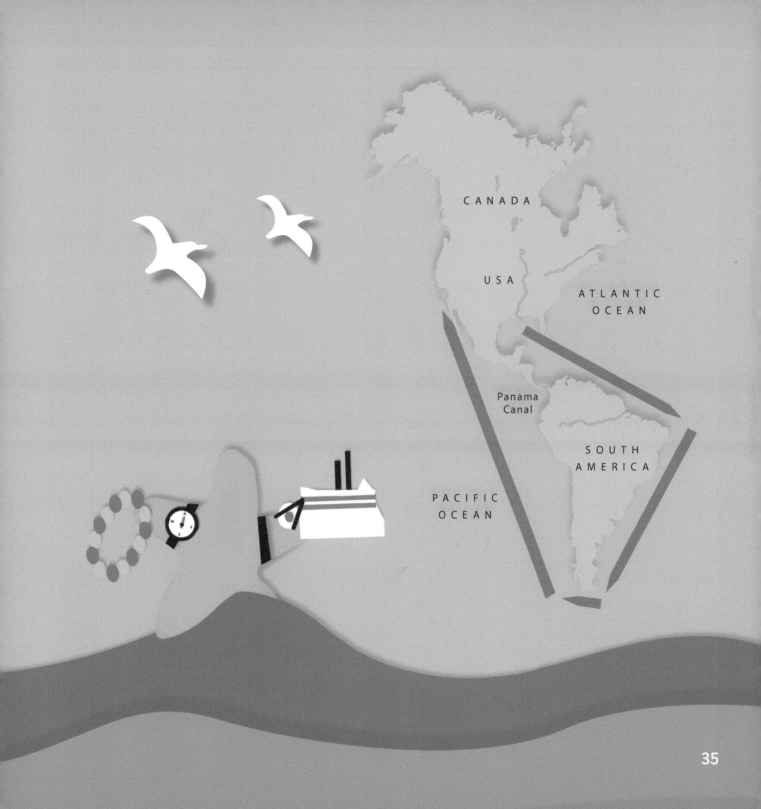

CANADA

USA

ATLANTIC
OCEAN

Panama
Canal

PACIFIC
OCEAN

SOUTH
AMERICA

The minute Shiny got home to the Santa Monica Pier, he rushed to the Library.

Ms. Muriel, Ms. Muriel, I just came back from the M-I-S-S-I-S-S-I-P-P-I River. I won a toy Paddlewheel Boat to add to my collection!

AND, I brought you some beads from the famous Mardi Gras Parade in New Orleans!

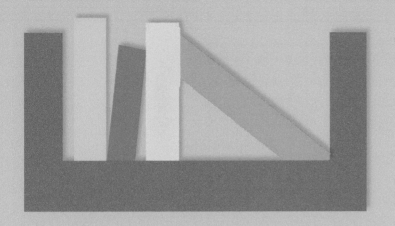

Welcome back, Shiny! Thank you so much!

I wonder what river adventure you will have next.

Many thanks to María Vélez, from Vélez Design, who turned my Shiny notebooks into shining books.

And to Christopher James Alexander of CJA Creative Collaborations, LLC, who introduced us.

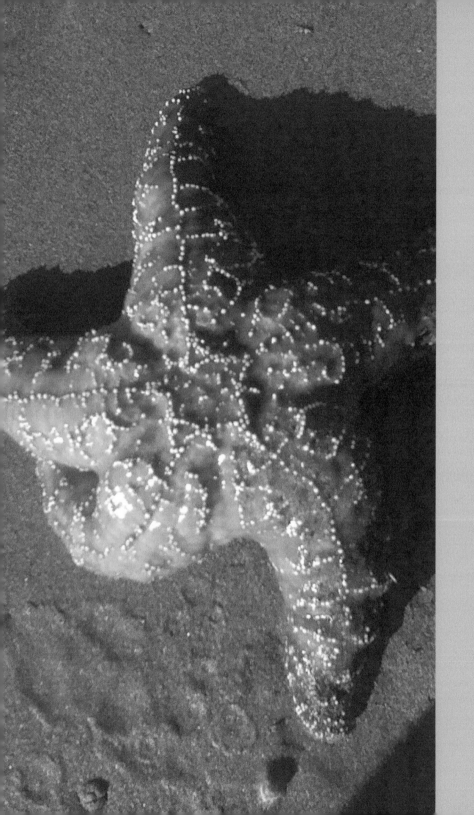

Shiny the Sea Star,
lives under the Santa
Monica Pier, in
Santa Monica,
California.

Cleopatra Bugelas Alexander has been a philanthropy consultant for more than 30 years.

Long committed to education issues, she served on the Board of Evanston/Skokie Elementary School District 65.

She is a graduate of Evanston Township High School and Carleton College.

An avid traveler, she resides in Evanston, Illinois and Santa Monica, California.

Mom! Mom!
Did you know that we can be friends
with the WHOLE WORLD, because we
are all connected by water? I can surf
across the water and stop at rivers and
make new friends EVERYWHERE!

Yes, Shiny. You have learned an
important lesson. We all share
the same water and we all can,
and should, be friends.

Which river will you visit next?

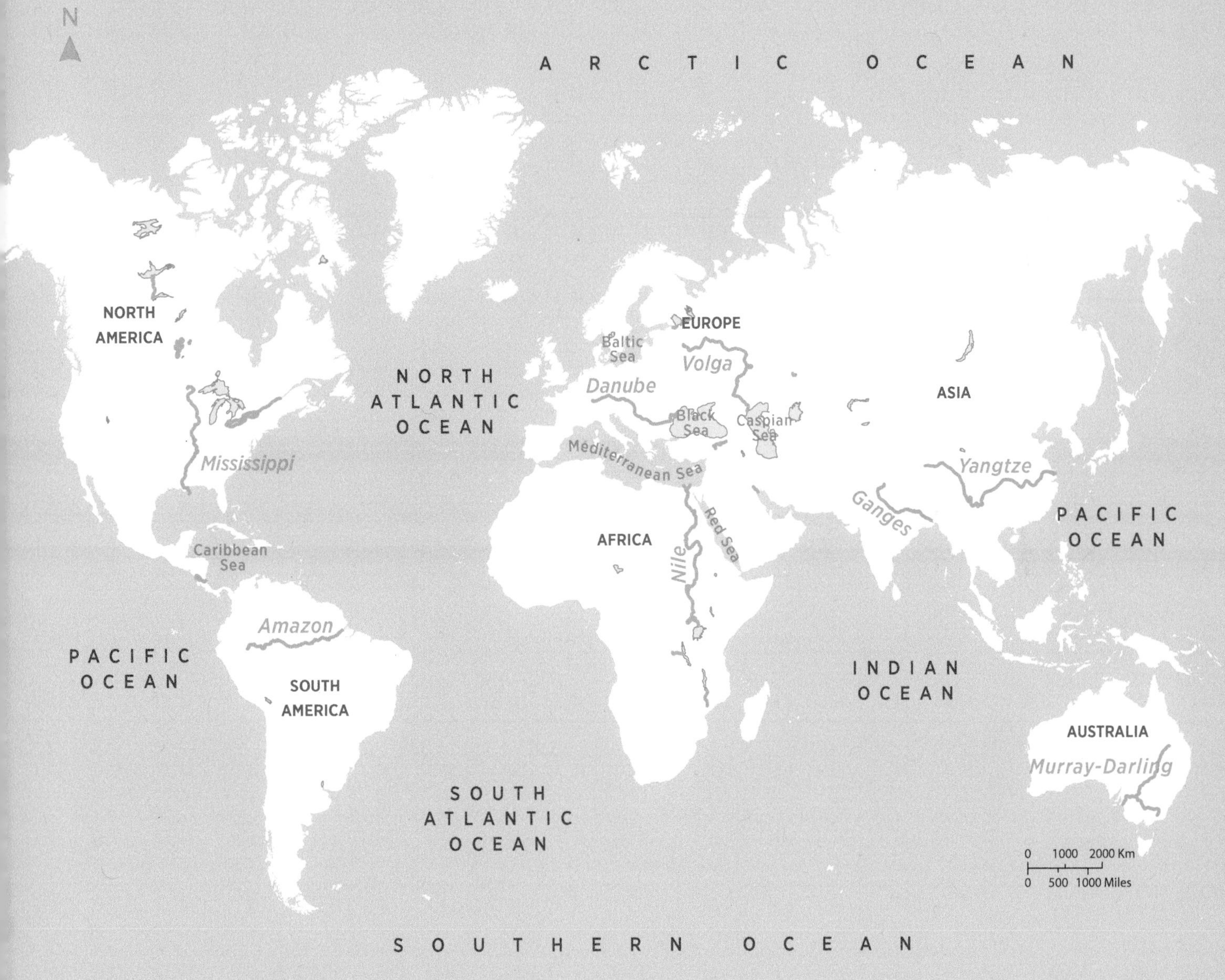
N
ARCTIC OCEAN
NORTH AMERICA
EUROPE
Baltic Sea
Volga
Danube
NORTH ATLANTIC OCEAN
Black Sea
Caspian Sea
ASIA
Mississippi
Mediterranean Sea
Yangtze
Red Sea
Ganges
PACIFIC OCEAN
AFRICA
Caribbean Sea
Nile
Amazon
PACIFIC OCEAN
SOUTH AMERICA
INDIAN OCEAN
AUSTRALIA
Murray-Darling
SOUTH ATLANTIC OCEAN
0 1000 2000 Km
0 500 1000 Miles
SOUTHERN OCEAN